illustrated by Harry Bishop

Illustrated Classics

BLACK BEAUTY

Anna Sewell

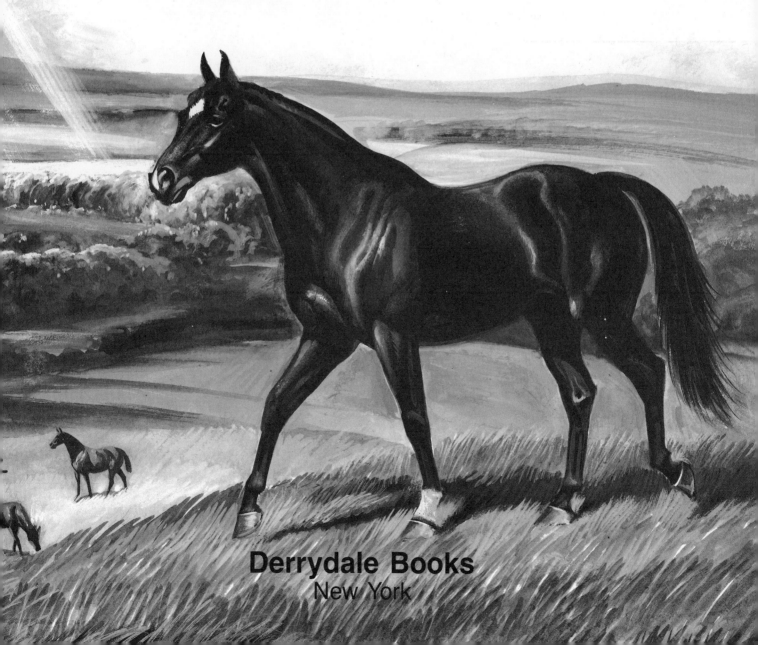

Derrydale Books
New York

My Early Home

The first place that I can remember was a large pleasant meadow with a pond of clear water in it. Some trees overshadowed the pond, and rushes and water-lilies grew at the deep end. Over the hedge on one side we looked into a ploughed field; and on the other, we looked over a gate at our master's house which stood by the roadside. At the top of the meadow was a plantation of fir-trees; and at the bottom, a running brook overhung by a steep bank.

Whilst I was young I lived upon my mother's milk, as I could not eat grass. In the daytime I ran by her side, and at night I lay down close by her. When it was hot, we used to stand by the pond in the shade of the trees; and when it was cold, we had a nice warm shed near the plantation.

There were six young colts in the meadow besides me. They were older than I was; some were nearly as large as grown-up horses. I used to run with them, and have great fun. We used to gallop all together round and round the field, as hard as we could go.

Mother had the sweetest temper of any horse I ever knew, and I think I have never seen her kick or bite.

"I hope you will grow up gentle and good, and never learn bad ways," she said to me one day. "Do your work with a good will; lift up your feet well when you trot, and never bite or kick even in play." I have never forgotten my mother's advice; I knew she was a wise old horse, and our master thought a great deal of her. Her name was Duchess, but he often called her Pet.

Old Daniel, the man who looked after the horses, was just as gentle as our master, so we were well off.

The Hunt

Before I was two years old, something happened which I have never forgotten.

The other colts and I were feeding in the lower part of the field when we heard, quite in the distance, what sounded like the cry of dogs.

"They are the hounds. They have found a hare," said my mother, "and if they come this way, we shall see the hunt. Look, there she is;" and just then a hare, wild with fright, rushed by, and made for the road.

Alas! it was too late; the dogs were upon her with their wild cries. We heard one shriek, and that was the end of her.

By the brook, two fine horses were down; one was struggling in the stream, and the other was groaning on the grass. One of the riders, covered with mud, was getting out of the water; the other lay quite still.

"His neck is broken," said my mother.

Many of the riders had gone to the young man; but my master, who had been watching what was going on, was the first to raise him. His head fell back and his arms hung down, and everyone looked very serious.

There was no noise now; even the dogs were quiet, and seemed to know that something was wrong.

When Mr Bond, the farrier, came to look at the

black horse that lay groaning on the grass, he felt him all over and shook his head; one of the horse's legs was broken. Then some one ran to our master's house and came back with a gun. Presently there was a loud bang and a dreadful shriek, and then all was still; the black horse moved no more.

My mother seemed much troubled. She said she had known that horse for years. His name was Rob Roy; a good bold horse with no vice in him. Afterwards she never would go to that part of the field.

Not many days after, we heard the church bell tolling for a long time; and looking over the gate we saw a long, strange, black coach covered with black cloth and drawn by black horses. After that came another, and another, and another; and all were black. Meanwhile the bell kept tolling, tolling. They were carrying young George Gordon, the Squire's only son, to the churchyard to bury him. He would never ride again, 'twas all for one little hare.

My Breaking In

I was now beginning to grow handsome; my coat had grown fine and soft, and was glossy black. I had one white foot, and a pretty white star on my forehead. People thought me very handsome.

When I was four years old, Squire Gordon came to look at me. He examined my eyes and my mouth, and felt my legs all down. Then I had to walk, trot, and gallop before him. He seemed to like me, and said, "When he has been well broken in, he will do very well." My master promised to break me in himself as he would not like me to be frightened or hurt; and he lost no time about it, for the next day the breaking in began.

Of course I had long been used to a halter and a headstall, and to be led about in the fields and lanes quietly, but now I was to have a bit and a bridle. What a nasty thing the bit was! Those who have never had one in their mouth cannot think how bad it feels. A great piece of cold, hard steel as thick as a man's finger is pushed between your teeth and over your tongue, with the ends coming out at the corners of your mouth, and is held fast there by straps over your head, under your throat, round your nose, and under your chin; so that no way in the world can you get rid of the nasty hard thing. Yes, very bad! At least, I thought so; but I knew my mother always wore one when she went out, and that all horses did when they were grown up. And so, what with the nice oats, and what with my master's pats, kind words, and gentle ways, I got to wear my bit and bridle.

Next came the saddle, but that was not nearly so bad, and within a few days I had grown quite used to it.

At length, one morning my master got on my back

and rode me round the meadow on the soft grass. It certainly did feel queer; but I must say I felt rather proud to carry my master; and, as he continued to ride me a little every day, I soon became accustomed to it.

The next unpleasant business was putting on the iron shoes; that too was very hard at first. My master went with me to the smith's forge to see that I was not hurt or frightened.

I must not forget to mention one part of my training which I have always considered a very great advantage. My master sent me for a fortnight to a neighbouring farmer who had a meadow which was skirted on one side by the railway. Here were some sheep and cows, and I was turned in amongst them.

I shall never forget the first train that ran by. I was feeding quietly near the pales which separated the meadow from the railway, when I heard a strange sound at a distance; and before I knew whence it came—with a rush and a clatter, and a puffing out of smoke—a long black trail of something flew by, and was gone almost before I could draw my breath. I turned, and galloped to the further side of the meadow as fast as I could go; and there I stood snorting with astonishment and fear.

I soon found that this terrible creature never came into the field nor did me any harm, so I began to disregard it; and very soon I cared as little about the passing of a train as the cows and sheep did.

My master often drove me in double harness with my mother because she was steady, and could teach me how to go better than a strange horse. She told me the better I behaved, the better I should be treated, and that it was wisest always to do my best to please my master.

"Do your best wherever you are, and keep up your good name."

Birtwick Park

At this time I used to stand in the stable, and my coat was brushed every day till it shone like a rook's wing. Early in May there came a man from Squire Gordon's, who took me away to the Hall. My master said, "Goodbye, Darkie; be a good horse, and always do your best." I could not say "Goodbye," so I put my nose into his hand; he patted me kindly, and then I left my first home.

Squire Gordon's park skirted the village of Birtwick. It was entered by a large iron gate, at which stood the first lodge; and then you trotted along on a smooth road between clumps of large old trees. Soon you passed another lodge and another gate, which brought you to the house and the gardens. Beyond this lay the home paddock, the old orchard and the stables. The stable into which I was taken was very roomy, with four good stalls. A large swinging window opened into the yard; this made it pleasant and airy.

When I had eaten my corn, I looked round. In the stall next to mine stood a little fat pony, with a thick mane and tail, a very pretty head, and a pert little nose.

Putting my head up to the iron rails at the top of my box, I said, "How do you do? What is your name?"

He turned round as far as his halter would allow, held up his head, and said: "My name is Merrylegs. I am very handsome. I carry the young ladies on my

back, and sometimes I take our mistress out in the low chair. They think a great deal of me, and so does James. Are you going to live next door to me in the box?"

"Yes," I replied.

The horse in the stable beyond looked ill-tempered; her ears were laid back. She was a tall chestnut mare, with a long, handsome neck.

"The thing is this," said Merrylegs. "Ginger has a bad habit of biting and snapping: that is why she is called Ginger. When she was in the loose box, she used to snap very much. One day she bit James in the arm and made it bleed, and so Miss Flora and Miss Jessie, who are very fond of me, were afraid to go into the stable. They used to bring me nice things to eat—an apple, or a carrot, or a piece of bread; but after Ginger stood in that box, they dared not come, and I miss them very much. I hope, if you do not bite or snap, that they will now come again."

I told him I never bit anything but grass, hay and corn, and could not think what pleasure Ginger found in it.

A Fair Start

The name of the coachman was John Manly. The next morning he took me into the yard and gave me a good grooming. Just as I was going into my box with my coat soft and bright, the Squire came in to look at me, and seemed pleased.

After breakfast John came and fitted me with a bridle. He was very particular in letting out and taking in the straps, to fit my head comfortably. Then he brought the saddle, which fitted nicely. He rode me at first slowly, then at a trot, and afterwards at a canter; and when we were on the common he gave me a light touch with his whip, and we had a splendid gallop.

As we came back through the park, we met the Squire and Mrs Gordon walking. They stopped, and John jumped off.

"Well, John, how does he go?"

"First-rate, sir," answered John. "He is as fleet as a deer."

"That's well," said the Squire. "I will try him myself tomorrow."

The next day I was brought up for my master. I remembered my mother's counsel and my good old master's, and I tried to do exactly what the Squire wanted me to do. I found he was a very good rider, and thoughtful for his horse, too. When we came home, the lady was at the Hall door as he rode up.

"Well, my dear," she said, "how do you like him?"

"He is exactly what John said, my dear. A pleasanter creature I never wish to mount. What shall we call him?"

"Would you like Ebony?" said she; "He is as black as ebony."

"No, not Ebony."

"Will you call him Blackbird, like your uncle's old horse?"

"No; he is far handsomer than old Blackbird ever was."

"Yes," she said, "he really is quite a beauty, and he has such a sweet, good-tempered face and such a fine, intelligent eye—what do you say to calling him Black Beauty?"

"Black Beauty—why, yes, I think that is a very good name. If you like, it shall be so," and that is how I got my name.

A few days after this I had to go in the carriage with Ginger. I wondered how we should get on together; but except laying her ears back when I was

led up to her, she behaved very well. She did her work honestly, and did her full share; and I never wish to have a better partner in double harness.

As for Merrylegs, he and I soon became great friends. He was such a cheerful, plucky, good-tempered little fellow that he was a favourite with everyone, and especially with Miss Jessie and Flora, who used to ride him about in the orchard and have fine games with him and their little dog Frisky.

12

Liberty

I was quite happy in my new place, and if there was one thing that I missed, it must not be thought I was discontented. All who had to do with me were good, and I had a light, airy stable and the best of food.

What more could I want? Why, liberty! For three years and a half of my life I had had all the liberty I could wish for; but now, week after week, month after month, and no doubt year after year, I must stand up in a stable night and day except when I am wanted; and then I must be just as steady and quiet as any old horse who has worked twenty years. I must wear straps here and straps there, a bit in my mouth, and blinkers over my eyes.

I ought to say that sometimes we had our liberty for a few hours; this used to be on fine Sundays in the summertime. The carriage never went out on Sundays, because the church was not far off.

It was a great treat to us to be turned out into the home paddock or the old orchard; the grass was so cool and soft to our feet; the air was so sweet, and the freedom to do as we liked— to gallop, lie down, roll over on our backs, or nibble the sweet grass— was so pleasant. Then, as we stood together under the shade of the large chestnut-tree, it was a very good time for talking.

Ginger

One day, when Ginger and I were standing alone in the shade, we had a long talk. She wanted to know all about my bringing up and breaking in; so I told her.

"Well," said she, "if I had had your bringing up I might have as good a temper as you; but now I don't believe I ever shall."

"Why not?" I said.

"Because it has been all so different with me," she replied. "I never had any one, horse or man, that was kind to me, or that I cared to please; for in the first place I was taken from my mother as soon as I was weaned, and put with a lot of other young colts; none of them cared for me, and I cared for none of them. But when it came to breaking in, that was a bad time for me. Several men came to catch me; and when at last they closed me in at one corner of the field, one caught me by the forelock, another took me by the nose, holding it so tight I could hardly draw my breath, and a third, grasping my under jaw in his hard hand, wrenched my mouth open; and so by force they got on the halter and put the bar into my mouth. Samson, my master, used to boast that he had never found a horse that could throw him. There was no gentleness in him as there was in his father, the old master, but only hardness: a hard voice, a hard eye and a hard hand. I felt from the first that what he wanted was to wear all the spirit out of me, and just make me into a quiet, humble, obedient piece of horse-flesh. 'Horse-flesh!' Yes, that is all that he thought about!" and Ginger stamped her foot as if the very thought of him made her angry.

"I felt my whole spirit set against him, and I began to kick, and plunge, and rear as I had never done before; we had a regular fight. For a long time he stuck to the saddle and punished me cruelly with his whip and spurs; but my blood was thoroughly up, and I cared for nothing he could do if only I could get him off.

"At last, after a terrible struggle, I threw him off backwards. I heard him fall heavily upon the turf, and without looking behind me, galloped off to the other end of the field; there I turned round and saw my persecutor slowly rise from the ground and go into the stable. I stood under an oak-tree and watched, but no one came to catch me. Later, hungry and thirsty, I walked towards the stable. Mr

Ryder—the old master—met me at the door.

"The skin was so broken at the corners of my mouth that I could not eat the hay, for the stalks hurt me. He looked closely at my mouth, shook his head, and told the man to fetch me a good bran mash and put some meal into it. How good that mash was, so soft and healing to my mouth. He stood by, stroking me and talking to the man all the time I was eating. 'If a high-mettled creature like this,' said he, 'can't be broken in by fair means, she never will be good for anything.'

"After that he often came to see me, and when my mouth was healed, the other breaker, Job, went on training me. As he was steady and thoughtful, I soon learned what he wanted."

Ginger's Story Continued

The next time that Ginger and I were together in the paddock, she told me about her first place.

"After my breaking in," she said, "I was bought by a dealer to match another chestnut horse. For some weeks he drove us together, and then we were sold to a gentleman, and were sent up to London."

"Did your new master take any thought for you?" I said.

"No," said she, "he cared only to have a stylish turnout, as they call it. I think he knew very little about horses; he left that to his coachman, who told him that I was of an irritable temper, and that I had not been well broken to the bearing rein, but that I

should soon get used to it.

"However, he was not the man to do it; for when I was in the stable, miserable and angry, instead of being soothed and quieted by kindness, I only got a surly word or a blow. If he had been civil, I would have tried to bear it. I was willing to work and ready to work hard too; but to be tormented for nothing but their fancies angered me. What right had they to make me suffer like that? Besides the soreness in my mouth and the pain in my neck, the bearing rein always made my windpipe feel bad; and if I had stopped there long, I know it would have spoiled my breathing.

"I grew more and more restless and irritable; I could not help it. Then I began to snap and kick when anyone came to harness me, and for this the groom beat me. One day, as they had just buckled us into the carriage and were straining my head up with that rein, I began to plunge and kick with all my might. I soon broke a lot of harness, and kicked myself clear; so my stay there was ended.

"Soon I was sent to Tattersall's to be sold. Of course I could not be warranted free from vice; so nothing was said about that. The dealer said he thought he knew a place where I should do well, and the end of it was that I came here not long before you did. I had now made up my mind that men were my natural enemies, and that I must defend myself. Of course it is very different here; but who knows how long it will last? I wish I could think about things as you do; but I can't after all I have gone through."

But Ginger began to improve. Master noticed the change too, and one day when he got out of the carriage and came to speak to us as he often did, he stroked her beautiful neck. "Well, my pretty one, how do things go with you now? You are a good bit happier than when you came to us, I think."

She put her nose up to him in a friendly, trustful way, while he rubbed it gently.

"We shall make a cure of her, John," he said.

"Yes, sir, she's wonderfully improved; she's not the same creature that she was. It's the Birtwick balls, sir," said John, laughing.

This was a little joke of John's; he used to say that a course of the Birtwick horse-balls would cure almost any vicious horse. These balls, he said, were made up of patience and gentleness, firmness and petting: one pound of each to be mixed with half a pint of common-sense, and given to the horse every day.

Merrylegs

Mr Blomefield, the Vicar, had a large family of boys and girls, who sometimes came to play with Miss Jessie and Flora. One of the girls was as old as Miss Jessie; two of the boys were older, and there were several little ones. When they came, there was plenty of work for Merrylegs, for nothing pleased them so much as getting on him in turn, and riding him all about the orchard and the home paddock by the hour together.

One afternoon he had been out with them a long time, and when James brought him in and put on his halter, he said:

"There, you rogue, mind how you behave yourself, or we shall get into trouble."

"What have you been doing, Merrylegs?" I asked.

"Oh!" said he, tossing his little head, "I have only been giving these young people a lesson. They did not know when they had had enough, nor when I had had enough; so I just pitched them off backwards: that was the only thing they could understand."

"What?" said I, "you threw the children off? I thought you knew better than that! Did you throw Miss Jessie or Miss Flora?"

He looked very much offended, and said:

"Of course not; I would not do such a thing for the best oats that ever came into the stable. Why, I am as careful of our young ladies as the master could be; and as for the little ones, it is I who teach them to ride. When they seem frightened or a little unsteady on my back, I go as smoothly and as quietly as old pussy when she is after a bird; and when they are all right, I go on again faster, just to use them to it. So don't you trouble yourself preaching to me; I am the best friend and riding master those children have.

"It is not they; it is the boys. Boys," said he, shaking his mane, "are quite different; they must be broken in, as we were broken in when we were colts, and must just be taught what's what.

"The other children had ridden me about for nearly two hours, and then the boys thought it was their turn; and so it was, and I was quite agreeable. They rode me in turn, and I galloped them about, up and down the fields and all about the orchard for a good hour.

"They had each cut a great hazel stick for a riding whip, and laid it on a little too hard; but I took it in good part, till at last I thought we had had enough; so I stopped two or three times by way of a hint. Boys, you see, think a horse or pony is like a steam engine or threshing machine, that can go on as long and as fast as they please. They never think that a pony can get tired, or have any feelings; so as the one whipping me could not understand, I just rose up on my hind legs and let him slip off behind – that was all."

18

A Talk in the Orchard

Ginger and I were not of the regular tall, carriage-horse breed; we had more of the racing blood in us. We stood about fifteen and a half hands high, and were therefore just as good for riding as for driving. Our master used to say that he disliked either horse or man that could do but one thing; and as he did not want to show off in London parks, he preferred a more active and useful kind of horse.

As for us, our greatest pleasure was when we were saddled for a riding party – the master on Ginger, the mistress on me, and the young ladies on Sir Oliver and Merrylegs. It was so cheerful to be trotting and cantering all together that it always put us in high spirits. I had the best of it, for I always carried the mistress. Her weight was little, her voice sweet, and her hand so light on the rein that I was guided almost without feeling it.

I had often wondered how it was that Sir Oliver, another of our master's horses, had such a very short tail; it really was only six or seven inches long, with a tassel of hair hanging from it; and on one of our holidays in the orchard, I ventured to ask him by what accident he had lost his tail.

"Accident!" he snorted, with a fierce look, "it was no accident! It was a cruel, shameful, cold-blooded act! When I was young I was taken to a place where these cruel things were done. I was tied up, and made fast so that I could not stir; and then they came and cut my long, beautiful tail through the flesh and through the bone, and took it away."

"How dreadful!" I exclaimed.

"Dreadful! Ah, it was dreadful, but it was not only the pain, though that was terrible and lasted a long time; it was not only the indignity of having my best ornament taken from me, though that was bad; but it was this – how could I ever again brush the flies off my sides and off my hind legs? You who have tails just whisk the flies off without thinking about it; and you can't tell what a torment it is to have them settle upon you, and sting and sting, and yet have nothing in the world with which to lash them off. I tell you it is a lifelong wrong, and a lifelong loss. But, thank Heaven! men don't do it now."

"What did they do it for then?" said Ginger.

"For fashion!" said the old horse, with a stamp of his foot. "For fashion! if you know what that means. There was not a well-bred young horse in my time that had not his tail docked in that shameful way, just as if the good God that made us did not know what we wanted and what looked best."

"I suppose it is fashion that makes them strap our heads up with those horrid bits that I was tortured with in London," said Ginger.

"Of course it is," said he. "To my mind, fashion is one of the most wicked things in the world. What right have they to torment and disfigure God's creatures?"

Sir Oliver, though he was so gentle, was a fiery old fellow; and what he said was all so new to me and so dreadful, that I found a bitter feeling toward men that I had never had before rise up in my mind. Of course, Ginger was much excited. With flashing eyes and distended nostrils, she flung up her head, declaring that men were both brutes and blockheads.

"Can any one tell me the use of blinkers?"

"No!" said Sir Oliver, shortly, "because they are no use."

"They are supposed," said Justice, our master's only other horse, "to prevent horses from shying and starting, and getting so frightened as to cause accidents."

"Then what is the reason they do not put them on riding horses, especially on ladies' horses?" said I.

"There is no reason at all," he said quietly, "except the fashion. Some years ago, I remember, there was a hearse with two horses returning one dark night, and just by Farmer Sparrow's house where the pond is close to the road, the wheels went too near the edge, and the hearse was overturned into the water. Both the horses were drowned, and the driver hardly escaped. Of course after this accident, a stout white rail was put up that might easily be seen; but if those horses had not been partly blinded, they would of themselves have kept farther from the edge, and no accident would have happened.

"When our master's carriage was overturned, before you came here, it was said that if the lamp on the left side had not gone out, John would have seen the great hole that the road-makers had left; and so he might. But if old Colin had not had blinkers on, he would have seen it, lamp or no lamp, for he was far too knowing an old horse to run into danger. As it was, he was very much hurt, the carriage was broken, and how John escaped nobody knew."

"The master," put in Merrylegs, "said that if horses had been used to them, it might be dangerous in some cases to leave them off; and John said he thought it would be a good thing if all colts were

broken in without blinkers, as was done in some foreign countries; so let us cheer up and have a run to the other end of the orchard. I believe the wind has blown down some apples, and we may just as well eat them ourselves as leave them for the slugs to have them all."

Merrylegs' suggestions could not be resisted; so we broke off our long conversation and got up our spirits by munching some very sweet apples which lay scattered on the grass.

A Stormy Day

One day, late in the autumn, my master had a long journey to go on business. I was put into the dog-cart, and John went with his master. I always liked to go in the dog-cart, it was so light, and the high wheels ran along so pleasantly. There had been a great deal of rain, and now the wind was very high and blew the dry leaves across the road in a shower. We went merrily along till we came to the toll-bar and the low wooden bridge. The river banks were rather high and the bridge, instead of rising, went across just level, so that in the middle, if the river was full, the water would be nearly up to the woodwork and planks; but as there were good substantial rails on each side, people did not mind it.

The man at the gate said the river was rising fast, and he feared it would be a bad night. Many of the meadows were under water, and in one low part of

the road the water was half-way up to my knees; the bottom was good, and master drove gently, so it was no matter.

When we got to the town, of course I had a good bait; but as the master's business engaged him a long time, we did not start for home till rather late in the afternoon. The wind was then much higher, and I heard the master say to John he had never been out in such a storm; and so I thought, as we went along the skirts of a wood, where the great branches were swaying about like twigs, and the rushing sound of the wind through the trees was terrible.

"I wish we were well out of this wood," said my master.

"Yes, sir," said John, "it would be rather awkward if one of these branches came down upon us."

The words were scarcely out of his mouth, when

there was a groan, a crack, and a splitting sound, and tearing, crashing down amongst the other trees, came an oak, torn up by the roots, which fell right across the road just before us. I will never say I was not frightened, for I was. I stopped still, and I believe I trembled. Of course, I did not turn round or run away; I was not brought up to do that. John jumped out and in a moment was at my head.

"That was a very near touch," said my master. "What's to be done now?"

"Well, sir, we can't drive over that tree nor yet get round it; there will be nothing for it but to go back to the four cross-ways, and that will be a good six miles before we get round to the wooden bridge again. It will make us late, but the horse is fresh."

So back we went, and round by the cross roads; but by the time we got to the bridge, it was very nearly dark, and we could just see that the water was over the middle of it; but as that happened sometimes when the floods were out, master did not stop.

We were going along at a good pace, but the moment my feet touched the first part of the bridge, I felt sure there was something wrong. I dare not go forward, and so I made a dead stop. "Go on Beauty," said my master, giving me a touch with the whip; but I dare not stir. He gave me a sharp cut; I jumped, but I dared not go forward.

"There's something wrong, sir," said John; and he sprang out of the dog-cart and came to my head and looked all about. He tried to lead me forward. "Come on, Beauty, what's the matter?" Of course I could not tell him, but I knew very well that the bridge was not safe.

Just then the man at the toll-gate on the other side ran out of the house, tossing a torch about like one mad.

"Hoy, hoy, hoy, halloo, stop!" he cried.

"What's the matter?" shouted my master.

"The bridge is broken in the middle, and part of it is carried away; if you come on you'll be into the river."

"Thank God!" said my master. "You Beauty!" said John; and taking the bridle he gently turned me round to the right-hand road by the river side. The sun had set some time, the wind seemed to have lulled off after that furious blast which tore up the tree. It grew darker and darker, and more and more still. I trotted quietly along, the wheels hardly making a sound on the soft road.

24

James Howard

One morning, early in December, John had just led me into my box after my daily exercise, and was strapping my cloth on. James was coming in from the corn-chamber with some oats, when the master came into the stable. He looked rather serious, and held an open letter in his hand. John fastened the door of my box, touched his cap, and waited for orders.

"Good morning, John," said the master; "I want to know if you have any complaint to make of James?"

"Complaint, sir? No, sir."

"Is he industrious at his work and respectful to you?"

"Yes, sir, always."

"You never find he slights his work when your back is turned?"

"Never, sir."

"James, my lad," said the master, "set down the oats and come here. I am very glad to find that John's opinion of your character agrees so exactly with my own. John is a cautious man," he said, with a droll smile, "and it is not always easy to get his opinion about people; so I thought if I beat the bush on this side, the birds would fly out, and I should learn what I wanted to know quickly; so now we will come to business.

"I have a letter from my brother-in-law, Sir Clifford Williams of Clifford Hall. He wants me to find him a trustworthy young groom, about twenty or twenty-one, who knows his business.

"How old are you, James?" said master.

"Nineteen next May, sir."

"That's young. What do you think, John?"

"Well, sir, it is young; but he is as steady as a man, strong, and well grown; and though he has not had much experience in driving, he has a light, firm hand, a quick eye, and is very careful. I am quite sure no horse of his will be ruined for want of having his feet and shoes looked after."

In a few days after this conversation, it was fully settled that James should go to Clifford Hall in a month or six weeks as it best suited his master, and in the meantime he was to get all the practice in driving that could be given him.

I never knew the carriage go out so often before. When the mistress did not go out, the master usually drove himself in the two-wheeled chaise; but now, whether it was master or the young ladies who wanted to go out, or whether it was only an errand had to be done, Ginger and I were put into the carriage and James drove us. At first, John rode with him on the box, telling him this and that, and afterwards James drove alone.

The Old Ostler

My master and mistress decided to pay a visit to some friends who lived about forty-six miles from our home, and James was to drive them. The first day we travelled thirty-two miles; there were some long, heavy hills, but James drove so carefully and thoughtfully that we were not at all harassed. He never forgot to put on the drag as we went downhill, nor to take it off at the right place. He kept our feet on the smoothest part of the road; and if the uphill was very long, he set the wheels a little across the road so that the carriage should not run back, and gave us breathing time.

We stopped once or twice on the road; and just as the sun was going down, we reached the town where we were to spend the night. We stopped at the principal hotel, a very large one in the Market Place. We drove under an archway into a long yard, at the further end of which were the stables and coach-houses. Two ostlers came to take us out. The head ostler was a pleasant, active little man, with a crooked leg and a yellow striped waistcoat. I never saw a man unbuckle harness so quickly as he did; and then with a pat and a good word he led me to a long stable with six or eight stalls in it and two or three horses. The other man brought Ginger—James stood by whilst we were rubbed down and cleaned.

I never was cleaned so lightly and quickly as by that little old man. When he had done, James stepped up and felt me over, as if he thought I could not be thoroughly done; but he found my coat as clean and smooth as silk.

"Well," he said, "I thought I was pretty quick, and our John quicker still, but you do beat all I ever saw for being quick and thorough at the same time."

"Practice makes perfect," said the crooked little ostler, "and 'twould be a pity if it didn't. Forty years' practice, and not perfect! Ha! ha! that would be a pity. As to being quick, why, bless you, that is only a matter of habit. If you get into the habit of being quick, it is just as easy as being slow—easier I should say. In fact, it does not agree with my health to be hulking about over a job twice as long as it need take. Bless you! I couldn't whistle if I crawled over my work as some folks do.

"You see, I have been about horses ever since I was twelve years old, in hunting stables and racing stables. Being small, you see, I was a jockey for several years; but at the Goodwood the turf was very

26

slippery and my poor Larkspur got a fall, and I broke my knee; and so of course I was of no more use there.

"But I could not live without horses, of course I couldn't, so I took to the hotels; and I can tell you it is a downright pleasure to handle an animal like this; well-bred, well mannered, well-cared-for. Bless you! I can tell how a horse is treated. Give me the handling of a horse for twenty minutes, and I'll tell you what sort of a groom he has had.

"Look at this one, pleasant, quiet, turns about just as you want him to do, holds up his feet to be cleaned out, or anything else you please to wish. Then you'll find another, fidgety, fretful, won't move the right way, or starts across the stall, tosses up his head as soon as you come near him, lays back his ears, and seems afraid of you, or else squares about at you with his heels.

"Poor things! I know what sort of treatment they have had. If they are timid, the treatment makes them vicious or dangerous; their tempers are mostly made when they are young. Bless you! They are like children; train 'em up in the way they should go, as the good Book says, and when they are old they will not depart from it—if they have a chance, that is."

The Fire

Later on in the evening, a traveller's horse was brought in by the second ostler, and whilst he was cleaning him, a young man with a pipe in his mouth lounged into the stable to gossip.

"I say, Towler," said the ostler to him, "just run up the ladder into the loft and bring down some hay into this horse's rack, will you? Only first lay down your pipe."

"All right," said the other, and went up through the trap door; and I heard him step across the floor overhead and put down the hay. James came in to look at us the last thing, and then the door was locked.

I cannot say how long I had slept, nor what time in the night it was, but I woke up feeling very uncomfortable, though I hardly knew why. I got up: the air seemed all thick and choking. I heard Ginger coughing, and one of the other horses moved about restlessly. It was quite dark, and I could see nothing; but the stable was full of smoke, and I hardly knew how to breathe.

The trap door had been left open, and I thought that was the place from which the smoke came. I listened and heard a soft, rushing sort of noise, and a low crackling and snapping. I did not know what it was, but there was something in the sound so strange that it made me tremble all over. The other horses were now all awake; some were pulling at their halters, others were stamping.

At last I heard steps outside, and the ostler who had put up the traveller's horse burst into the stable with a lantern, and began to untie the horses, and try to lead them out; but he seemed in such a hurry, and was so frightened himself, that he frightened me still more. The first horse would not go with him; he tried the second and third, but they too would not stir. He came to me next and tried to drag me out of the stall by force; of course that was no use. He tried us all by turns and then left the stable.

No doubt we were very foolish, but danger seemed to be all round; there was nobody whom we knew to trust in, and all was strange and uncertain. The fresh air that had come in through the open door made it easier to breathe, but the rushing sound overhead grew louder, and as I looked upward, through the bars of my empty rack, I saw a red light flickering on the wall. Then I heard a cry of "Fire!" outside, and the old ostler came quietly and quickly in. He got one horse out, and went to another; but the flames were playing round the trap door, and the roaring overhead was dreadful.

The next thing I heard was James's voice, quiet and cheery, as it always was.

"Come, my beauties, it is time for us to be off, so

29

wake up and come along." I stood nearest the door, so he came to me first, patting me as he came in.

"Come, Beauty, on with your bridle, my boy, we'll soon be out of this smother." It was on in no time; then he took the scarf off his neck, and tied it lightly over my eyes and, patting and coaxing, he led me out of the stable. Safe in the yard, he slipped the scarf off my eyes, and shouted, "Here, somebody! Take

this horse while I go back for the other.''

A tall, broad man stepped forward and took me, and James darted back into the stable. I set up a shrill whinny as I saw him go. Ginger told me afterwards that whinny was the best thing I could have done for her, for had she not heard me outside, she would never have had courage to come out.

At first no one could guess how the fire had been caused; but at last a man said he saw Dick Towler go into the stable with a pipe in his mouth, and when he came out he had not one, and went to the tap for another.

James said the roof and floor had all fallen in, and that only the black walls were standing. The two poor horses that could not be got out were buried under the burnt rafters and tiles.

John Manly's Talk

The rest of our journey was very easy, and a little after sunset we reached the house of my master's friend. We were taken into a clean, snug stable, where there was a kind coachman, who made us very comfortable. He seemed to think a great deal of James when he heard about the fire.

then returned home. All went well on the journey: we were glad to be in our own stable again, and John was equally glad to see us.

Before James and he left us for the night, James said, "I wonder who is coming in my place."

"Little Joe Green at the Lodge," said John.

"Little Joe Green! Why, he's a child!"

The next day Joe came to the stables to learn all he could before James left. He learned to sweep the stable, to bring in the straw and hay, and began to clean the harness, and help to wash the carriage. As he was quite too short to do anything in the way of grooming Ginger and me, James taught him upon Merrylegs, for, under John, he was to have full charge of the pony. He was a nice little bright fellow, and always came whistling to his work.

Merrylegs was a good deal put out at being "mauled about," as he said, "by a boy who knew nothing"; but towards the end of the second week he told me confidentially that he thought the boy would turn out well.

At last the day came when James had to leave us; cheerful as he always was, he looked quite down-hearted that morning.

"You see," he said to John, "I am leaving a great deal behind—my mother and Betsy, you, a good master and mistress, and the horses and my old Merrylegs. At the new place there will not be a soul I shall know. If it were not that I shall get a higher place, and be able to help my mother better, I don't think I should have made up my mind to it; it is a real pinch, John."

"Ay, James, lad, so it is, but I should not think much of you if you could leave your home for the first time and not feel it. Cheer up! you'll make friends there, and if you get on well—as I am sure you will—it will be a fine thing for your mother, and she will be proud enough that you have got into such a good place as that."

So John cheered him up, but everyone was sorry to lose James. As for Merrylegs, he pined after James for several days, and went quite off his appetite. So when he exercised me, John took him out several mornings with a leading rein, and trotting and galloping by my side he got up the little fellow's spirits again, and Merrylegs was soon all right.

Joe's father, Thomas, would often come in and give a little help, as he understood the work, and Joe took a great deal of pains to learn, and John was quite encouraged about him.

"There is one thing quite clear, young man," he said. "Your horses know whom they can trust. It is one of the hardest things in the world to get horses out of a stable when there is either fire or flood. I don't know why they won't come out, but they won't —not one in twenty."

We stopped two or three days at this place and

Going for the Doctor

One night, a few days after James had left, I had eaten my hay and was lying down in my straw fast asleep, when I was suddenly awakened by the stable bell ringing very loudly. I heard the door of John's house opened and his feet running up to the Hall. He was back again in no time. He unlocked the stable door and came in, calling out, "Wake up, Beauty, you must go well now, if ever you did!" and almost before I could think, he had placed the saddle on my back and the bridle on my head. He just ran round for his coat, and then took me at a quick trot up to the Hall door. The Squire stood there with the lamp in his hand.

"Now, John," he said, "ride for your life—that is, for your mistress's life; there is not a moment to lose. Give this note to Doctor White. Give your horse a rest at the inn, and be back as soon as you can."

John said, "Yes, sir," and was on my back in a minute.

There was before us a long piece of level road by the riverside. John said to me, "Now, Beauty, do your best," and so I did; I wanted neither whip nor spur, and for two miles I galloped as fast as I could lay feet to the ground.

The air was frosty, the moon bright, and it was very pleasant. We went through a village, through a dark wood, then uphill, then downhill, till after an eight miles' run we came to the town. On through the streets we went and into the Market Place. All was quite still except for the clatter of my feet on the stones—everybody was asleep. The church clock struck three as we drew up at Doctor White's door.

John rang the bell twice, and then knocked at the door like thunder. A window was thrown up, and Doctor White, in his nightcap, put his head out and said, "What do you want?"

"Mrs Gordon is very ill, sir; master wants you to come at once; he thinks she will die if you cannot get there—here is a note."

"Wait," he said, "I will come."

He shut the window and was soon at the door.

"The worst of it is," he said, "that my horse has been out all day and is quite done up; my son has just been sent for and he has taken the other. What is to be done? Can I have your horse?"

"He has come at a gallop nearly all the way, sir, and I was to give him a rest here, but I think my master would not be against it if you think fit, sir."

"All right," he said, "I will soon be ready."

I will not describe our way back; the doctor was a heavier man than John, and not so good a rider; however, I did my best.

I was glad to get home; my legs shook under me, and I could only stand and pant. I had not a dry hair on my body, the water ran down my legs, and I steamed all over—Joe used to say, like a pot on the fire. Poor Joe! he was young and small, and as yet he knew very little, and his father, who would have helped him, had been sent to the next village; but I am sure he did the very best he knew.

He rubbed my legs and my chest, but he did not put my warm cloth on me; he thought I was so hot I should not like it. Then he gave me a pailful of water to drink. It was cold, and very good, and I drank it all; then he gave me some hay and some corn, and thinking he had done right, he went away.

Soon I began to shake and tremble, and turned deadly cold; my legs, loins and chest ached, and I felt sore all over. Oh! how I wished for my warm, thick cloth as I stood and trembled. I wished for John, but he had eight miles to walk, so I lay down in my straw and tried to go to sleep.

After a long while I heard John at the door; I gave a low moan, for I was in great pain. He was at my side in a moment, stooping down by me. I could not tell him how ill I felt; but he seemed to know it all. He covered me up with two or three warm cloths,

and then ran to the house for some hot water; then he made me some warm gruel, which I drank; then, I think I went to sleep.

I was now very ill; a strong inflammation had attacked my lungs, and I could not draw my breath without pain. John nursed me night and day. He would get up two or three times in the night to come to me; my master, too, often came to see me. "My poor Beauty," he said one day, "my good horse, you saved your mistress's life! Yes, you saved her life."

Only Ignorance

I do not know how long I was ill. Mr Bond, the horse doctor, came every day. One day he bled me, and John held a pail for the blood. I felt very faint after it, and thought I should die. I believe they all thought so, too.

Ginger and Merrylegs had been moved into the other stable, so that I might be quiet, for the fever made me very quick of hearing; any little noise seemed quite loud, and I could tell everyone's footstep going to and from the house. I knew all that was going on. One night John had to give me a draught; Thomas Green came in to help him.

After I had taken it and John had made me as comfortable as he could, he said he should stay half an hour to see how the medicine settled. Thomas said he would stay with him, so they went and sat down on a bench that had been brought into Merrylegs' stall, and put down the lantern at their feet that I might not be disturbed with the light.

For a while both men sat silent, and then Tom Green said in a low voice:

"I wish, John, you'd say a bit of a kind word to my poor son Joe; the boy is quite broken-hearted; he can't eat his meals, and he can't smile. He says he knows it was all his fault, though he is sure he did

the best he knew; and he says, if Beauty dies, no one will ever speak to him again. It goes to my heart to hear him; I think you might give him just a word, he is not a bad boy.''

After a short pause, John said slowly: "You must not be too hard upon me, Tom. I know he meant no harm; I never said he did. I know he is not a bad boy, but you see I am sore myself. That horse is the pride of my heart, to say nothing of his being such a favourite with the master and mistress; and to think that his life may be flung away in this manner is more than I can bear. But if you think I am hard on the boy, I will try to give him a good word tomorrow —that is, I mean, if Beauty is better.''

"Well, John! thank you, I knew you did not wish to be too hard, and I am glad you see it was only ignorance.''

John's voice almost startled me as he answered, "Only ignorance! Only ignorance! How can you talk about only ignorance? Don't you know that ignorance is the worst thing in the world, next to wickedness?—and which does the most mischief Heaven only knows. If people can say, 'Oh! I did not know, I did not mean any harm,' they think it is all right.''

I heard no more of this conversation, for the medicine took effect and sent me to sleep, and in the morning I felt much better; but I often thought of John's words when I came to know more of the world.

Joe Green

Joe Green went on very well; he learned quickly, and was so attentive and careful that John began to trust him in many things; but, as I have said, he was small for his age, and it was seldom that he was allowed to exercise either Ginger or me. But it so happened one morning that John was out with Justice in the luggage cart, and the master wanted a note to be taken immediately to a gentleman's house about three miles distant, and sent his orders for Joe to saddle me and take it, adding the caution that he was to ride carefully.

The note was delivered, and we were quietly returning till we came to the brickfield. Here we saw a cart heavily laden with bricks. The wheels had stuck fast in the stiff mud of some deep ruts; and the carter was shouting and flogging the two horses unmercifully. Joe pulled up. It was a sad sight. There were the two horses straining and struggling with all their might to drag the cart out, but they could not move it. The sweat streamed from their legs and flanks, their sides heaved, and every muscle was strained, whilst the man, fiercely pulling at the head of the forehorse, swore and lashed most brutally.

"Hold hard," said Joe, "don't go on flogging the horses like that; the wheels are so stuck that they cannot move the cart." The man took no heed, but

40

continued to lash his horses.

"Stop! pray stop," said Joe; "I'll help you to lighten the cart, they can't move it now."

"Mind your own business, you impudent young rascal, and I'll mind mine." The man was in a towering passion and the worse for drink; and so he laid on the whip again. Helplessly, Joe galloped back home.

"Why, what's the matter with you, Joe? You look angry all over," said John, as the boy flung himself from the saddle.

"I am angry all over, I can tell you," said the boy, and then in hurried excited words he told all that had happened. Joe was usually so quiet and gentle that it was wonderful to see him so roused.

They were just going home to dinner when the footman came down to the stable to say that Joe was wanted directly in master's private room; there was a man brought up for ill-using horses, and Joe's evidence was wanted. The boy flushed up to his forehead, and his eyes sparkled. "They shall have it," said he.

It was wonderful what a change had come over Joe. John laughed, and said he had grown taller in that week; and I believe he had. He was just as kind and gentle as before, but there was more purpose and determination in all that he did—as if he had jumped at once from a boy into a man.

The Parting

I had now lived in this happy place three years, but sad changes were about to come over us. We heard from time to time that our mistress was ill. The Doctor was often at the house, and the master looked grave and anxious. Then we heard that she must leave her home at once and go to a warm country for two or three years. The news fell upon the household like the tolling of a death-bell. Everybody was sorry; but the master began directly to make arrangements for breaking up his establishment and leaving England. We used to hear it talked about in our stable; indeed, nothing else was talked about.

John went about his work silent and sad, and Joe scarcely whistled. There was a great deal of coming and going; Ginger and I had full work.

The first to go were Miss Jessie and Miss Flora with their governess. They came to bid us goodbye. They hugged poor Merrylegs like an old friend, and so indeed he was. Then we heard what had been been arranged for us. Master had sold Ginger and me to his old friend the Earl of W———, for he thought we should have a good place there. Merrylegs he had given to the Vicar, who was wanting a pony for Mrs Blomefield; but it was on the condition that he should never be sold, and that when he was past work he should be shot and buried.

Joe was engaged to take care of him and to help in the house; so I thought that Merrylegs was well off. John had the offer of several good places, but he said he should wait a little and look round.

Earlshall

The next morning after breakfast, Joe put Merrylegs into the mistress's low chaise to take him to the Vicarage. He came first and said goodbye to us, and Merrylegs neighed to us from the yard. Then John put the saddle on Ginger and the leading rein on me, and rode us across the country about fifteen miles to Earlshall Park, where the Earl of W——— lived.

We went into the yard through a stone gateway, and John asked for Mr York. It was some time before he came. He was a fine-looking, middle-aged man, and his voice said at once that he expected to be obeyed. He was very friendly and polite to John; and after giving us a slight look, he called a groom to take us to our boxes, and invited John to take some refreshment.

We were taken to a light, airy stable and placed in boxes adjoining each other, where we were rubbed down and fed. In about half an hour John and Mr York, who was to be our new coachman, came in to see us.

Afterwards John came to say goodbye. He came round to each of us to pat and speak to us for the last time; his voice sounded very sad.

I held my face close to him, as that was all I could do to say goodbye; and then he was gone, and I have never seen him since.

The next day Lord W——— came to look at us; he seemed pleased with our appearance.

"I have great confidence in these horses," he said, "from the character my friend Mr Gordon has given me of them. Of course, they are not a match in colour, but my idea is that they will do very well for the carriage whilst we are in the country. Before we go to London I must try to match Baron; the black horse, I believe, is perfect for riding."

At three o'clock we were at the door. We heard the silk dress rustle as the lady came down the steps, and in an imperious voice she said, "York, you must put those horses' heads higher; they are not fit to be seen."

York got down and said very respectfully, "I beg your pardon, my lady, but these horses have not been reined up for three years, and my lord said it would be safer to bring them to it by degrees; but if your ladyship pleases, I can take them up a little more."

"Do so," she said.

York came round to our heads and shortened the rein one hole, I think; every little makes a difference, be it for better or worse, and that day we had a steep hill to go up. Then I began to understand what I had heard. Of course, I wanted to put my head forward and take the carriage up with a will, as we had been used to do; but no, I had now to pull with my head up, and that took all the spirit out of me, and brought the strain on my back and legs.

Day by day, hole by hole, our bearing reins were shortened, and instead of looking forward with pleasure to having my harness put on as I used to do, I began to dread it. Ginger, too, seemed restless, though she said very little. At last I thought the worst was over; for several days there had been no more shortening, and I determined to make the best of it and to do my duty, though now going out was a constant harass instead of a pleasure; but the worst was yet to come.

A Strike for Liberty

One day my lady came down later than usual, and the silk rustled more than ever.

"Drive to the Duchess of B———'s," she said. Then, after a pause, she added, "Are you never going to get those horses' heads up, York? Raise them at once, and let us have no more of this humouring nonsense."

York came to me first, whilst the groom stood at Ginger's head. He drew my head back and fixed the rein so tight that it was almost intolerable; then he went to Ginger, who was impatiently jerking her head up and down against the bit, as was her way now. She had a good idea of what was coming, and the moment York took the rein off the terret in order to shorten it, she took her opportunity and reared up so suddenly that York had his nose roughly hit and his hat knocked off, and the groom was nearly thrown off his legs.

At once they both flew to her head, but she was a

match for them, and went on plunging, rearing and kicking in a most desperate manner. At last she kicked right over the carriage pole and fell down, after giving me a severe blow on my near quarter.

There is no knowing what further mischief she may have done had not York promptly sat himself down flat on her head to prevent her struggling, at the same time calling out, "Unbuckle the black horse! Run for the winch and unscrew the carriage pole; and somebody cut the trace if you can't unhitch it."

One of the footmen ran for the winch, and another brought a knife from the house. The groom set me free from Ginger and the carriage, and led me to my box. He just turned me in as I was, and ran back to York.

Before long, however, Ginger was led in by two grooms, a good deal knocked about and bruised. York came with her and gave his orders, and then came to look at me. In a moment he let down my head.

"Confound these bearing reins!" he said to himself. "I thought we should have some mischief soon."

Ginger was never put into the carriage again, but when her bruises were healed, one of Lord W——'s younger sons said he should like to have her; he was sure she would make a good hunter. As for me, I was obliged still to go in the carriage, and had a fresh partner, called Max, who had always been used to the tight rein. I asked him how it was he bore it.

"Well," he said, "I bear it because I must, but it is shortening my life, and it will shorten yours too if you have to stick to it."

What I suffered for four long months with that rein it would be hard to describe; but I am quite sure that, had it lasted much longer, either my health or my temper would have given way. Before that, I never knew what it was to foam at the mouth; but now the action of the sharp bit on my tongue and jaw, and the constrained position of my head and throat, always caused me to froth more or less at the mouth.

In my old home I always knew that John and my master were my friends; but here, although in many ways I was well treated, I had no friend. York might have known, and very likely did know, how that rein harassed me; but I suppose he took it as a matter of course that could not be helped; at any rate, nothing was done to relieve me.

Reuben Smith

I must now say a little about Reuben Smith, the other coachman, who was left in charge of the stables when York went to London. No one more thoroughly understood his business than he did, and when he was all right, there could not be a more faithful or valuable man. He was gentle and very clever in his management of horses, and could doctor them almost as well as a farrier, for he had lived two years with a veterinary surgeon. He was a first-rate driver, and could take a four-in-hand, or a tandem, as easily as a pair.

He was a handsome man, a good scholar, and had very pleasant manners. I believe everybody liked him; certainly the horses did. The only wonder was that he should be in an under situation, and not in the place of a head coachman like York: but he had one great fault—the love of drink. He was not like some men, always at it; he used to keep steady for weeks or months together; but then he would break out and have a "bout" of it, as York called it, and be a disgrace to himself, a terror to his wife, and a nuisance to all that had to do with him. He was, however, so useful that two or three times York had hushed the matter up and kept it from the Earl's knowledge.

It was now early in April, and the family was expected home some time in May. The light brougham was to be fresh done up, and as Colonel Blantyre, a cousin who had been staying at the Hall, was obliged to return to his regiment, it was arranged that Smith should drive him to the town in it, and then ride back; for this purpose he took the saddle with him, and I was chosen for the journey.

At the station the Colonel put some money into Smith's hand and bade him goodbye.

We left the carriage at the maker's, and Smith drove me to the 'White Lion', and ordered the ostler to feed me well and have me ready for him at four o'clock. A nail in one of my front shoes had loosened as I came along, but the ostler did not notice it till just about four o'clock. Smith did not come into the yard till five, and then he said he should not leave till six, as he had met with some old friends. The man then told him of the nail, and asked if he should have the shoe looked to.

"No," said Smith, "that will be all right till we get home."

He spoke in a very loud, offhand way, and I thought it was very unlike him not to see about the

shoe, as he was generally wonderfully particular about loose nails in our shoes. He came neither at six, seven, nor eight, and it was nearly nine o'clock before he called me; and then it was with a loud, rough voice. He seemed in a very bad temper and abused the ostler, though I could not tell what for.

If Smith had been in his right senses, he would have been sensible of something wrong in my pace; but he was too madly drunk to notice that I had lost one of my shoes.

Beyond the turnpike was a long piece of road, upon which some fresh stones had just been laid— large, sharp stones, over which no horse could be driven quickly without risk of danger. Over this road, with one shoe gone, I was forced to gallop at my utmost speed, my rider meanwhile cutting into me with his whip, and with wild curses urging me to go still faster. Of course my shoeless foot suffered

dreadfully; the hoof was broken and split down to the quick, and the inside was terribly cut by the sharpness of the stones.

This could not go on; no horse could keep his footing under such circumstances as the pain was too great. I stumbled, and fell with violence on both my knees. Smith was flung off by my fall and, owing to the speed at which I was going, he must have fallen with great force. I soon recovered my feet and limped to the side of the road, where it was free from stones.

The moon had just risen above the hedge, and by its light I could see Smith lying a few yards beyond me. After making one slight effort to rise, there was a heavy groan. He did not move. I could have groaned too, for I was suffering intense pain both from my foot and knees; but horses are used to bear their pain in silence. I uttered no sound, but stood there and listened.

How It Ended

It must have been nearly midnight when I heard at a great distance the sound of a horse's feet. Sometimes the sound died away, then it grew clearer again and nearer. The road to Earlshall led through plantations that belonged to the Earl; the sound came in that direction, and I hoped it might be someone coming in search of us. As the sound came nearer and nearer, I was almost sure I could distinguish Ginger's step; a little nearer still, and I could tell she was in the dog-cart. I neighed loudly, and was overjoyed to hear an answering neigh from Ginger and men's voices. They came slowly over the stones, and stopped at the dark figure that lay upon the ground.

One of the men jumped out, and stooped down over it. "It is Reuben!" he said, "and he does not stir."

The other man followed and bent over him. "He's dead," he said; "feel how cold his hands are."

They raised him up, but there was no life, and his hair was soaked with blood. Laying him down again, they came and looked at me and saw my cut knees.

"Hallo! he's bad in his foot as well as his knees. Look here—his hoof is cut all to pieces; he might well come down, poor fellow! I tell you what, Ned, I'm afraid it hasn't been all right with Reuben! Just think of him riding a horse over these stones without a shoe! Why, if he had been in his right senses, he would just as soon have tried to ride him over the moon. I'm afraid it has been the old thing over again."

At last I reached my own box and had some corn; and after Robert had wrapped up my knees in wet cloths, he tied up my foot in a bran poultice to draw out the heat, and to cleanse it before the horse doctor saw it in the morning. Then I managed to get myself

down on the straw and slept in spite of the pain.

As Smith's death had been so sudden, and no one was there to see it, there was an inquest held. The landlord and ostler at the 'White Lion', with several other people, gave evidence that he was intoxicated when he started from the inn; the keeper of the toll-gate said he rode at a hard gallop through the gate; and my shoe was picked up amongst the stones; so the case was quite plain to them, and I was cleared of all blame.

Ruined, and Going Downhill

As soon as my knees were sufficiently healed, I was turned into a small meadow for a month or two. No other creature was there, and though I enjoyed the liberty and the sweet grass, yet I had been so long used to society that I felt very lonely. Ginger and I had become fast friends, and now I missed her company extremely.

I often neighed when I heard horses' feet passing in the road, but seldom got an answer; till one morning the gate was opened, and who should come in but poor old Ginger! The man slipped off her halter and left her there. With a joyful whinny I trotted up to her; we were both glad to meet, but I soon found that it was not for our pleasure that she was brought to be with me. Her story would be too long to tell, but the end of it was that she had been ruined by hard riding, and was now turned off to see what rest would do.

"And so," she said, "here we are, ruined in the prime of our youth and strength—you by a drunkard, and I by a fool; it is very hard."

One day we saw the Earl come into the meadow, and York was with him. Seeing who it was, we stood still under our lime-tree, and let them come up to us. They examined us carefully. The Earl seemed much annoyed.

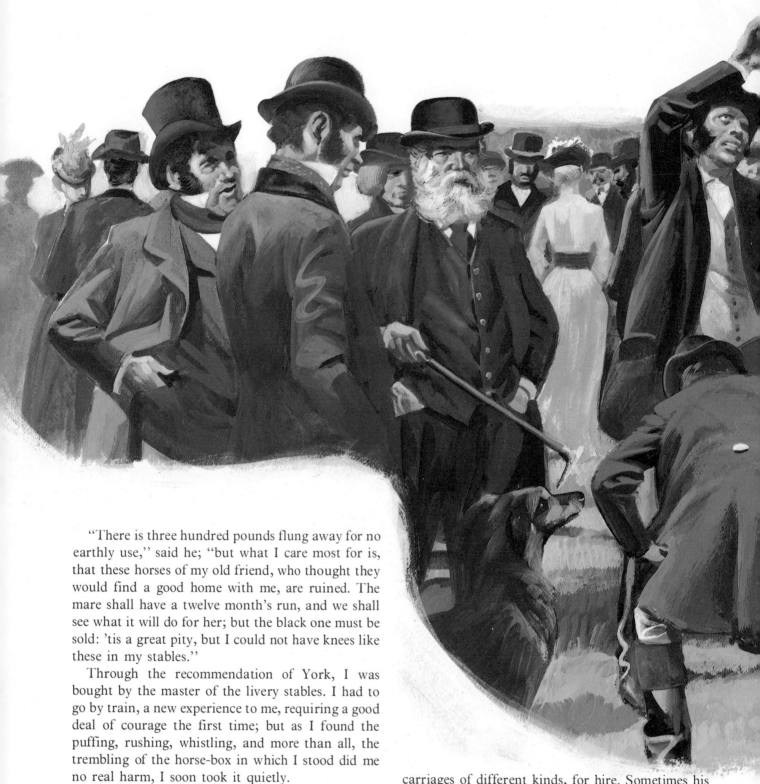

"There is three hundred pounds flung away for no earthly use," said he; "but what I care most for is, that these horses of my old friend, who thought they would find a good home with me, are ruined. The mare shall have a twelve month's run, and we shall see what it will do for her; but the black one must be sold: 'tis a great pity, but I could not have knees like these in my stables."

Through the recommendation of York, I was bought by the master of the livery stables. I had to go by train, a new experience to me, requiring a good deal of courage the first time; but as I found the puffing, rushing, whistling, and more than all, the trembling of the horse-box in which I stood did me no real harm, I soon took it quietly.

When I reached the end of my journey, I found myself in a tolerably comfortable stable and well attended to. I was well fed and well cleaned and, on the whole, I think our master took as much care of us as he could. He kept a good many horses and carriages of different kinds, for hire. Sometimes his own men drove them; at others the horse and chaise were let to gentlemen or ladies who drove themselves.

I did not stay here long, but was soon taken to the horse fair to be sold again.

A Horse Fair

No doubt a horse fair is a very amusing place to those who have nothing to lose; at any rate, there is plenty to see—long strings of young horses out of the country, fresh from the marshes; droves of shaggy little Welsh ponies, no higher than Merrylegs; hundreds of cart horses of all sorts, some of them with their long tails braided up and tied with scarlet cord; and a good many, like myself, handsome and high-bred, but fallen into the middle class through some accident or blemish, unsoundness of wind, or some other complaint.

There were some splendid animals quite in their prime and fit for anything, who were throwing out their legs and showing off their paces in high style as they were trotted out with a leading rein, the groom running by the side. But round in the background were a number of poor things, sadly broken down with hard work, their knees knuckling over, and their hind legs swinging out at every step; some were very dejected-looking old horses, with the upper lip hanging down and the ears lying back heavily, as if there was no pleasure in life and no more hope; again, some were so thin you could see all their ribs; and some had old sores on their backs and hips. These were sad sights for a horse who knows not but that he may come to the same sad state.

There was a great deal of bargaining, running up and beating down; and if a horse may speak his mind so far as he understands, I should say there were more lies told and more trickery carried on at that horse fair than a clever man could give account of.

There was one man of whom I thought that if he would buy me I should be happy. He was not a gentleman, nor yet one of the loud, flashy sort that called themselves so. He was a rather small man, but well made, and quick in all his motions. I knew in a moment by the way he handled me that he was used to horses; he spoke gently, and his grey eye had a kindly, cheery look in it. It may seem strange—but it is true all the same—that the clean, fresh smell there was about him made me take to him. There was no smell of old beer and tobacco, which I hated, but a fresh smell as if he had come out of a hay-loft. He offered twenty-three pounds for me; but that was refused.

"Well, old chap," he said, "I think we should suit each other. I'll give twenty-four for him."

"Say twenty-five and you shall have him."

"Twenty-four ten," said my friend, in a very

decided tone, "and not another sixpence—yes or no?"

"Done," said the salesman, "and you may depend upon it there's a monstrous deal of quality in that horse, and if you want him for cab work, he's a bargain."

The money was paid on the spot, and my new master took my halter and led me out of the fair to an inn, where he had a saddle and bridle ready. He gave me a good feed of oats, and stood by whilst I ate it, talking to himself and talking to me. Half an hour after we were on our way to London. We reached the great city at twilight and soon turned up one of the side streets. About half-way up we turned again into a very narrow one, with rather poor-looking houses on one side and what seemed to be coach-houses and stables on the other.

My owner pulled up at one of the houses and whistled. The door flew open, and a young woman, followed by a little girl and boy, ran out. There was a very lively greeting as my rider dismounted.

"Now then, Harry, my boy, open the gates, and mother will bring us the lantern."

The next minute they were all standing round me in a small stable yard.

"Is he gentle, father?"

"Yes, Dolly, as gentle as your own kitten; come and pat him. We'll call him Jack, after the old one, shall we, Dolly?"

At once the little hand was patting about fearlessly all over my shoulder. How good it felt!

"Let me get him a bran mash while you rub him down," said the mother.

"Do, Polly, it's just what he wants, and I know you've got a beautiful mash ready for me."

"Sausage dumpling and apple turnover," shouted the boy: this set them all laughing. I was led into a comfortable, clean-smelling stall with plenty of dry straw and, after a capital supper, I lay down, thinking I was going to be happy.

A London Cab Horse

My new master's name was Jeremiah Barker, but as every one called him Jerry, I shall do the same.

Jerry had a cab of his own and two horses, which he drove and attended to himself. His other horse was a tall, white, rather large-boned animal, called Captain. He was fairly old now, but when he was young he must have been splendid; there was still the proud way of holding his head and arching his neck; in fact, he was a high-bred, fine mannered, noble old horse, every bit of him. He told me that in his early youth he went to the Crimean War, for he belonged to an officer in the cavalry, and used to lead the regiment. He said he quite enjoyed the training with all the other horses—trotting together, turning together to the right hand or the left, halting at the word of command, or dashing forward at full speed at the sound of the trumpet or signal of the officer.

When young, he was a dark, dappled iron grey, and was considered very handsome. His master, a young, high-spirited gentleman, was very fond of him, and from the first treated him with the greatest care and kindness. He told me he thought the life of an army horse was very pleasant; but when it came to being sent abroad in a great ship over the sea, he almost changed his mind.

"But what about the fighting?" said I; "was not that worse than anything else?"

"Well," said he, "I hardly know. We always liked to hear the trumpet sound, and to be called out, and were impatient to start off, though sometimes we had to stand for hours, waiting for the word of command. But when the word was given, we used to spring forward as gaily and eagerly as if there were no cannon-balls, bayonets or bullets. I believe so long as we felt our rider firm in the saddle, and his hand steady on the bridle, not one of us gave way to fear, not even when the terrible bombshells whirled through the air and burst into a thousand pieces.

"With my master, I went into many actions without a wound; and though I saw horses shot down with bullets, others pierced through with lances or gashed with fearful sabre-cuts, though I left them dead on the field, or dying in the agony of their wounds, I don't think I feared for myself. My master's cheery voice as he encouraged his men made me feel as if he and I could not be killed. I had

such perfect trust in him that whilst he was guiding me, I was ready to charge up to the very cannon's mouth.

"Do you know what they fought about?" said I.

"No," said he, "that is more than a horse can understand; but the enemy must have been awfully wicked people if it was right to go all the way over the sea on purpose to kill them."

Jerry Barker

I never knew a better man than my new master — kind and good, as strong for the right as John Manly, and so good-tempered and merry that very few people could pick a quarrel with him. He was very fond of making little songs, which he would sing to himself. His favourite was this:

> "Come, father and mother,
> And sister and brother,
> Come, all of you, turn to
> And help one another."

And so they did; Harry was as clever at stable-work as a much older boy, and always wanted to do what he could. Then Polly and Dolly used to come in the morning to help with the cab—to brush and beat the cushions and rub the glass, while Jerry was giving us a cleaning in the yard and Harry was cleaning the harness. There used to be a great deal of laughing and fun between them, and it put Captain and me in much better spirits than if we had heard scolding and hard words.

Although Jerry was steadfastly set against hard driving to please careless people, he always went at a good fair pace, and was not against putting on the steam, as he said, if only he knew why.

Poor Ginger

One day, whilst our cab and many others were waiting outside one of the parks where a band was playing, a shabby old cab drove up beside ours. The horse was an old worn out chestnut with an ill-kept coat, and with bones that showed plainly through it. The knees knuckled over, and the forelegs were very unsteady.

I had been eating some hay, and the wind rolling a little lock of it that way, the poor creature put out her long, thin neck and picked it up, and then turned round and looked about for more. There was a hopeless look in the dull eye that I could not help noticing; and then, as I was thinking where I had seen that horse before, she looked full at me and said, "Black Beauty, is that you?"

It was Ginger – but how changed! The beautifully arched and glossy neck was now straight, lank and fallen in; the clean, straight legs and delicate fetlocks were swollen; the joints were grown out of shape with hard work; the face that was once so full of spirit and life was now full of suffering; and I could tell by the heaving of her sides and by her frequent cough how bad her breath was.

Our drivers were standing together a little way off, so I sidled up to her a step or two that we might

have a little quiet talk. It was a sad tale that she had to tell.

After a twelve month's run off at Earlshall, she was considered to be fit for work again, and was sold to a gentleman. For a little while she got on very well, but after a longer gallop than usual, the old strain returned and, after being rested and doctored, she was again sold. In this way she changed hands several times, but always getting lower down.

"And so at last," said she, "I was bought by a man who keeps a number of cabs and horses, and lets them out. You look well off, and I am glad of it; but I cannot tell you what my life has been. When they found out my weakness, they said I was not worth what they gave for me, and that I must go into one of the low cabs and just be used up; that is what they are doing – whipping and working me, with never one thought of what I suffer. They paid for me, and must get the money out of me, they say. The man who hires me now pays a deal of money to the owner every day, and so he has to get it out of me first; and so it goes on all the weeks round, with never a Sunday rest."

I said, "You used to stand up for yourself if you were ill-used."

"Ah!" she said, "I did once, but it's no use; men are stronger, and if they are cruel and have no feeling, there is nothing that we can do but just bear it – bear it on and on to the end. I wish the end was come; I wish I was dead. I have seen dead horses, and I am sure they do not suffer pain; I hope I may drop down dead at my work, and not be sent off to the knacker's."

I was very much troubled, and I put my nose up to hers, but I could say nothing to comfort her. I think she was pleased to see me, for she said, "You are the only friend I ever had."

Just then her driver came up, and with a tug at her mouth backed her out of the line and drove off, leaving me very sad indeed.

A short time after this, a cart with a dead horse in it passed our cab-stand. The head hung out of the cart tail, the lifeless tongue was slowly dripping blood; and the sunken eyes! – but I can't speak of them, the sight was too dreadful. It was a chestnut horse with a long, thin neck. I saw a white streak down the forehead. I believe it was Ginger; I hoped it was, for then her troubles would be over. Oh! if men were more merciful, they would shoot us before we come to such misery.

Jerry's New Year

Christmas and the New Year are very merry times for some people; but for cabmen and cabmen's horses these times are no holiday, though they may be a harvest. There are so many parties, balls and places of amusement open that the work is hard and often late. Sometimes driver and horse, shivering with cold, have to wait for hours in the rain or frost, whilst the merry people within are dancing to the music. I wonder if the beautiful ladies ever think of the weary cabman waiting on his box, and of his patient beast standing till his legs get stiff with cold!

We had a great deal of late work in the Christmas week, and Jerry had a bad cough but, however late we were, Polly sat up for him and, looking anxious and troubled, she came out with the lantern to meet him.

On the evening of the New Year we had to take two gentlemen to a house in one of the West End squares. We set them down at nine o'clock and were told to come again at eleven. "But," said one of them, "as it is a card party, you may have to wait a few minutes, but don't be late."

As the clock struck eleven we were at the door, for Jerry was always punctual. The clock chimed the quarters – one, two, three, and then struck twelve; but the door did not open.

The wind had been very changeable, with squalls of rain during the day, but now it came on sharp, driving sleet, which seemed to come all the way round one; it was very cold, and there was no shelter. Jerry got off his box and came and pulled one of my cloths a little more over my neck; then, stamping his feet, he took a turn or two up and down; then, he began to beat his arms, but that set him on coughing; so he opened the cab door and sat at the bottom with his feet on the pavement, and was thus a little sheltered. Still the clock chimed the quarters, but no one came. At half past twelve he rang the bell, and asked the servant if he would be wanted that night.

"Oh! yes, you'll be wanted safe enough," said the man; "you must not go, it will soon be over." And again Jerry sat down, but his voice was so hoarse I could hardly hear him.

At a quarter past one the door opened, and the two gentlemen came out; they got into the cab without a word, and told Jerry where to drive; it was nearly two miles away. My legs were numb with cold, and I thought I should have stumbled. When the men got out, they never said they were sorry to have kept us waiting so long, but were angry at the charge. However, as Jerry never charged more than was his due, he never took less, and so they had to pay for the two hours and a quarter waiting; but it was hard-earned money to Jerry.

At last we got home. He could hardly speak, and his cough was dreadful. Polly asked no questions, but opened the door and held the lantern for him.

"Can't I do something?" she said.

"Yes; get Jack something warm, and then boil me some gruel."

This was said in a hoarse whisper. He could hardly get his breath, but he gave me a rub down as usual, and even went up into the hay-loft for an extra bundle of straw for my bed. Polly brought me a warm mash that made me comfortable; and then they locked the door.

It was late the next morning before any one came, and then it was only Harry. He cleaned and fed us, and swept out the stalls; then he put the straw back again as if it was Sunday. He was very still, and neither whistled nor sang. At noon he came again and gave us our food and water: this time Dolly came with him. She was crying, and I could gather from what they said that Jerry was dangerously ill, and the doctor said it was a bad case. So two days passed, and there was great trouble indoors. We saw only Harry and sometimes Dolly. I think she came for company, for Polly was always with Jerry, who had to be kept very quiet.

On the third day, whilst Harry was in the stable, a tap came at the door, and kindly Governor Grant came in.

He was a prosperous cab-owner who had a great many horses which were hired out to drivers for so much money per day.

"I wouldn't go to the house, my boy," he said, "but I want to know how your father is."

"He is very bad," said Harry, "he can't be much worse. They call it bronchitis, and the doctor thinks it will turn one way or another tonight."

"That's bad, very bad," said Governor Grant, shaking his head. "I know two men who died of that last week. It takes 'em off in no time; but whilst there's life there's hope, so you must keep up your spirits."

"Yes," said Harry quickly, "and the doctor said that father had a better chance than most men, because he didn't drink. He said yesterday the fever

was so high that if father had been a drinking man, it would have burnt him up like a piece of paper; but I believe he thinks he will get over it; don't you think he will, Mr Grant?"

The Governor looked puzzled.

"If there's any rule that good men should get over these things, I am sure he will, my boy. He's the best man I know. I'll look in early tomorrow."

Early next morning, he was there.

"Well?" said he.

"Father is better," said Harry. "Mother hopes he will get over it."

Governor Grant

"Thank God!" said the Governor; "and now you must keep him warm, and keep his mind easy. And that brings me to the horses. You see, Jack will be all the better for the rest of a week or two in a warm stable, and you can easily take him a turn up and down the street to stretch his legs; but this young one, if he does not get work, will soon be all up on end as you may say, and will be rather too much for you; and when he does go out, there'll be an accident."

"He is like that now," said Harry; "I've kept him short of corn, but he's so full of spirit I don't know what to do with him."

"Just so," said Governor Grant. "Now look here. Will you tell your mother that, if she is agreeable, I will come for him every day till something is arranged, and take him for a good spell of work; and whatever he earns, I'll bring your mother half of it, and that will help with the horses' feed. Your father is in a good club, I know, but that won't keep the horses, and they'll be eating their heads off all this time: I'll come at noon to hear what she says"; and without waiting for Harry's thanks, he picked up his coat and was gone.

At noon I think he went and saw Polly, for Harry and he came to the stable together, harnessed Captain, and took him out.

For a week or more he came for Captain, and when Harry thanked him or said anything about his kindness, he laughed it off, saying, it was all good luck for him, for his horses were wanting a little rest which they could not otherwise have had.

Jerry steadily grew better, but the doctor said that he must never go back to the cab-work again if he wished to be an old man. The children had many consultations together about what father and mother would do, and how they could help to earn money to keep the horses.

One afternoon Captain was brought in very wet and dirty.

"The streets are nothing but slush," said the Governor; "it will give you a good warming, my boy, to get him clean and dry."

"All right, Governor," said Harry, "I shall not leave him till he is; you know I have been trained by my father."

"I wish all the boys had been trained like you," said the Governor.

On the Move Again

While Harry was sponging off the mud from Captain's body and legs, Dolly came in, looking very full of something.

"Who lives at Fairstowe, Harry? Mother has got a letter from Fairstowe; she seemed so glad, and ran upstairs to father with it."

"Don't you know? Why, it is the name of Mrs Fowler's place – mother's old mistress, you know – the lady that father met last summer; who sent you and me five shillings each."

"Oh! Mrs Fowler; of course I know all about her. I wonder what on earth she can be writing to mother about."

"Mother wrote to her last week," said Harry. "You know she told father if ever he gave up the cab-work, she would like to know. I wonder what she says; run in and see, Dolly."

Harry scrubbed away at Captain with a "Huish! huish!" like any old ostler.

In a few minutes, Dolly came dancing into the stable.

"Oh, Harry! was there ever anything so beautiful? Mrs Fowler says we are all to go and live near her. There is a cottage now empty that will just suit us, with a garden, a hen-house, apple trees, and everything! Her coachman is going away in the spring, and then she will want father to look after the horses in his place. And there are good families round, where you can get a place in the garden or stable, or as a page-boy; and there's a good school for me. Mother is laughing and crying by turns, and father does look so happy!"

"That's uncommon jolly," said Harry, "and just the right thing, I should say. It will suit father and mother both; but I don't intend to be a page-boy with tight clothes and rows of buttons. I'll be a groom or a gardener."

It was quickly settled that, as soon as Jerry was well enough, they should remove to the country, and that the cab and horses should be sold as soon as possible.

This was heavy news for me, for I was not young now, and could not look for any improvement in my condition. Since I left Birtwick I had never been so happy as with my dear master, Jerry; but three years of cab-work, even under the best conditions, will tell on one's strength, and I felt that I was not the horse I had been.

Governor Grant said at once that he would take Captain. There were men in the stand who would have bought me; but Jerry said I should not go to cab-work again with just anybody, and the Governor promised to find a place for me where I should be comfortable.

The day came for going away. Jerry had not been allowed to go out yet, and I never saw him after that New Year's Eve. Polly and the children came to bid me goodbye. "Poor old Jack! dear old Jack! I wish we could take you with us," she said; and then, laying her hand on my mane, she put her face close to my neck and kissed me. Dolly was crying and she kissed me, too. Harry stroked me a great deal, but said nothing, only he seemed very sad; and so I was led away to my new place.

Hard Times

I shall never forget my new master. Skinner had a low set of cabs and a low set of drivers; he was hard on the men, and the men were hard on the horses. My driver was just as hard as his master. My life now was so utterly wretched that I wished I might, like Ginger, drop down dead at my work, and so be out of my misery; and one day my wish very nearly came to pass.

I went on the stand at eight in the morning, and had done a good share of work when we had to take a fare to the railway. A long train was just expected in, so my driver pulled up at the back of some of the outside cabs to take the chance of a return fare. It was a very heavy train, and as all the cabs were soon engaged, ours was called for.

There was a party of four: a noisy, blustering man with a lady, a little boy, a young girl, and a great deal of luggage. The lady and the boy got into the cab, and while the man ordered about the luggage,

the young girl came and looked at me.

"Papa," she said, "I am sure this poor horse cannot take us and all our luggage so far; he is so very weak and worn out; do look at him."

'Oh! he's all right, miss," said my driver, "he's strong enough."

The porter, who was pulling about some heavy boxes, suggested to the gentleman that, as there was so much luggage, he should take a second cab.

"Can your horse do it, or can't he?" said the blustering man.

"Oh! he can do it all right, sir. Send up the boxes, porter; he can take more than that." Saying this, he helped to haul up a box so heavy that I could feel the springs go down.

"Papa, papa, do take a second cab," said the young girl in a beseeching tone; "I am sure we are wrong; I am sure it is cruel."

"Nonsense, Grace, get in at once, and don't make all this fuss; a pretty thing it would be if a man of business had to examine every cab-horse before he hired it—the man knows his own business of course: there, get in and hold your tongue!"

My gentle friend had to obey; and box after box was dragged up and lodged on the top of the cab, or settled by the side of the driver. At last all was ready, and with his usual jerk of the rein and slash of the whip, he drove out of the station. I got along fairly till we came to Ludgate Hill; but there, the heavy load and my own exhaustion were too much. I was struggling to keep on, goaded by constant chucks of the rein and use of the whip, when, in a single moment—I cannot tell how—my feet slipped from under me, and I fell heavily to the ground on my side. The suddenness and the force with which I fell seemed to beat all the breath out of my body.

I lay perfectly still; indeed, I had no power to move, and I thought now I was going to die.

Someone came and loosened the throat strap of my bridle, and undid the traces which kept the collar so tight upon me. Someone said, "He's dead, he'll never get up again."

I cannot tell how long I lay there, but I found my life coming back, and a kind-voiced man was patting me and encouraging me to rise. After some cordial had been given me, and after one or two attempts, I staggered to my feet, and was gently led to some stables which were close by. Here I was put into a well-littered stall, and some warm gruel was brought to me: this I drank thankfully.

In the evening I was sufficiently recovered to be led back to Skinner's stables, where I think they did the best for me they could. In the morning Skinner came with a farrier to look at me. He examined me very closely, and said:

"This is a case of overwork more than disease, and if you could give him a run off for six months, he would be able to work again; but now there is not an ounce of strength in him."

"Then he must go to the dogs," said Skinner. "I have no meadows to nurse sick horses in."

"If he was broken-winded," said the farrier, "you had better have had him killed out of hand, but he is not; there is a sale of horses coming off in about ten days; if you rest him and feed him up, he may pick up, and you may at any rate get more than his skin is worth."

Upon this advice Skinner, rather unwillingly, I think, gave orders that I should be well fed and cared for; and the stableman, happily for me, carried out the orders with a much better will than his master had shown in giving them.

Ten days of perfect rest, plenty of good oats, hay, and bran mashes with boiled linseed mixed in them, did more to get up my condition than anything else could have done. Those linseed mashes were delicious, and I began to think that after all it might be better to live than go to the dogs. When the twelfth day after the accident came, I was taken to the sale, a few miles out of London. I felt that any change from my present place must be an improvement; so I held up my head, and hoped for the best.

Farmer Thoroughgood and His Grandson Willie

At this sale, of course, I found myself in company with the old broken-down horses—some lame, some broken-winded, some old, and some that I am sure it would have been merciful to shoot.

Coming from the better part of the fair, I noticed a man who looked a gentleman farmer, with a young boy by his side. He had a broad back and round shoulders, a kind, ruddy face, and he wore a broad-brimmed hat. When he came up to me and my companions, he stood still and gave a pitiful look round upon us. I saw his eye rest on me; I had still a good mane and tail, which did something for my appearance. I pricked my ears and looked at him.

"There's a horse that has known better days."

"Poor old fellow!" said the boy. "Do you think, grandpapa, he was ever a carriage horse?"

"Oh, yes, my boy," said the farmer, coming closer, "He might have been anything when he was young. Look at his nostrils and his ears, and the shape of his neck and shoulders; there's a deal of breeding about that horse." He put out his hand and gave me a kind pat on the neck. I put out my nose in answer to his kindness, and the boy stroked my face.

"Poor old fellow! See, grandpapa, how well he understands kindness. Could you not buy him and make him young again, as you did Ladybird?"

The farmer slowly felt my legs, which were much swollen and strained; then he looked at my mouth—"Thirteen or fourteen, I should say. Just trot him out, will you?"

I arched my poor thin neck, raised my tail a little and threw out my legs as well as I could, for they were very stiff.

"What is the lowest you will take for him?" said the farmer as I came back.

"Five pounds, sir; that was the lowest price my master set."

I was bought and taken to a large meadow. Perfect rest, good food, soft turf and gentle exercise soon began to tell on my condition and my spirits. I

had a good constitution from my mother, and I was never strained when I was young, so that I had a better chance than many horses who have been worked before they came to their full strength.

"He's growing young, Willie; we must give him a little gentle work now, and by midsummer he will be as good as Ladybird; he has a beautiful mouth and good paces; these could not be better."

"Oh, grandpapa, how glad I am you bought him!"

"So am I, my boy, but he has to thank you more than me. We must now be looking out for a quiet, genteel place for him where he will be valued."

My Last Home

One day during this summer the groom cleaned and dressed me with such extraordinary care that I thought some new change must be at hand. He trimmed my fetlocks and legs, passed the tarbrush over my hoofs, and even parted my forelock. I think the harness also had an extra polish. Willie seemed half anxious, half merry, and he got into the chaise with his grandfather.

"If the ladies take to him," said the old gentleman, "they'll be suited, and he'll be suited: we can but try."

At the distance of a mile or two from the village we came to a pretty, low house with a lawn and shrubbery at the front and a drive up to the door.

"You see, ladies," said Mr Thoroughgood, when they appeared, "many first rate horses have had their knees broken through the carelessness of their drivers, without any fault of their own; and from what I see of this horse, I should say that is his case: but of course I do not wish to influence you. If you wish, you can have him on trial, and then your coachman will see what he thinks of him."

"You have always been such a good adviser to us about our horses," said the stately lady, "that your recommendation would go a long way with me, and if my sister Lavinia sees no objection, we will accept with thanks your offer of a trial."

It was then arranged that I should be sent for the next day.

In the morning a smart-looking young man came for me. At first he looked pleased, but when he saw my knees, he said in a disappointed voice, "I didn't think, sir, you would have recommended my ladies a blemished horse like this."

"Handsome is that handsome does," said my master. "You are only taking him on trial, and I am sure you will do fairly by him, young man; and if he is not as safe as any horse you ever drove, send him back."

I was led home, placed in a comfortable stable, fed and left to myself. The next day, when my new groom was cleaning my face, he said, "That is just like the star that Black Beauty had, and he is much the same height too; I wonder where he is now?"

A little farther on he came to the place in my neck where I was bled, and where a little knot was left in the skin. He almost started, and began to look me over carefully, talking to himself.

"White star in the forehead, one white foot on the off side, this little knot just in that place;" then, looking at the middle of my back—"and as I am alive, there is that little patch of white hair that John used to call 'Beauty's threepenny-bit.' It must be Black Beauty! Why, Beauty! Beauty! do you know me, little Joe Green that almost killed you?"

And he began patting me and patting me as if he was quite overjoyed.

I could not say that I remembered him, for now he was a fine grown young fellow with black whiskers and a man's voice, but I was sure he knew me, and that he was Joe Green; so I was very glad. I put my nose up to him, and tried to say that we were friends. I never saw a man so pleased.

"Give him a fair trial! I should think so indeed! I wonder who the rascal was that broke your knees, my old Beauty! You must have been really badly served out somewhere. Well, well, it won't be my fault if you haven't good times of it now. I wish John Manly were here to see you."

I have now lived in this happy place a whole year. Joe is the best and kindest of grooms. My work is easy and pleasant, and I feel my strength and spirits all coming back again. Mr Thoroughgood said to Joe the other day, "In your place he will last till he is twenty years old—perhaps more."

Willie always speaks to me when he can, and treats me as his special friend. My ladies have promised that I shall never be sold, and so I have nothing to fear; and here my story ends. My troubles are all over and I am at home; and often before I am quite awake, I fancy I am still in the orchard at Birtwick, standing with my old friends under the apple trees.